128

ARCTIC
FOXES

ARCTIC
FOXES

BY DOWNS MATTHEWS

PHOTOGRAPHS BY

DAN GURAVICH
NIKITA OVSYANIKOV

SIMON & SCHUSTER
BOOKS FOR YOUNG READERS

Also by Downs Matthews
and Dan Guravich

Arctic Summer

Polar Bear Cubs

Skimmers

Wetlands

SIMON & SCHUSTER BOOKS FOR YOUNG READERS
An imprint of Simon & Schuster Children's Publishing Division
1230 Avenue of the Americas, New York, New York 10020
Text copyright © 1995 by Downs Matthews.
Photographs copyright © 1995 by Dan Guravich and Nikita Ovsyanikov.
SIMON & SCHUSTER BOOKS FOR YOUNG READERS
is a trademark of Simon & Schuster. Book design by Paul Zakris.
The text for this book is set in 13-point Versailles light.
Manufactured in the United States of America
10 9 8 7 6 5 4 3 2 1

Library of Congress Cataloging-in-Publication Data
Matthews, Downs.   Arctic foxes / by Downs Matthews ;
photographs by Dan Guravich and Nikita Ovsyanikov.
p. cm.
1. Arctic fox—Juvenile literature. [1. Arctic fox. 2. Foxes.]
I. Guravich, Dan, ill. II. Ovsyanikov, Nikita, ill. III. Title.
QL737.C22M365 1995 599.74'442—dc20   94-6012 CIP AC
ISBN: 0-689-80284-6

Dedicated to life and freedom
for all wild foxes everywhere

In the faraway Arctic, the sun doesn't rise in winter or set in summer. Cold, dry winds and frozen ground make life hard for plants and animals. But this is where arctic foxes live. The land of snow and ice around the North Pole is their home.

The arctic fox is a canine, related to dogs, coyotes, and wolves. But the arctic fox needs special advantages to help him survive in the far north.

The arctic fox has one of the warmest fur coats in nature. He has a thick, warm undercoat of fur that he wears like winter underwear. On top of that, he has a heavy overcoat of long hair to ward off snow and cold winds. His ears are small and covered with fur. He has furry feet like a rabbit's so that he can walk safely on slippery ice, and his feet won't freeze in the snow. Scientists call him the rabbit-footed fox. He has a long, bushy tail that he wraps around his body like a muffler to keep out the cold.

In winter the arctic fox grows white fur to match the snow. In his snowy world, he is hard to see. In summer when the snow melts, he sheds his warm, white fur and grows a cooler summer coat of brown and tan. Now he is hard to spot on bare rocky ground. Because his colors help him hide, the arctic fox can creep up on his prey. His colors also help him hide from larger animals that might want to eat him. No other member of the canine family can change its colors like this.

Once in a great while an arctic fox is born that does not grow a white coat in the wintertime. This fox keeps its dark coat throughout the year and is called a blue fox.

Arctic foxes are small compared to most other canines. Adults usually weigh between six and ten pounds. But their fur is so thick and bushy that they look much larger and heavier than they really are.

Like their canine cousins, arctic foxes are social animals. They live together in a den as a family group. The den must be in a mound so that it will stay dry. There must be a supply of fresh water nearby. A den may be very large. It may have many tunnels and rooms and holes that foxes can use to go in and out. Foxes like to use the same den year after year. When a pair of foxes dies, another pair of foxes moves in. Some arctic fox dens may have been used for thousands of years.

A male arctic fox is called a dog fox. A female fox is called a vixen. Their babies are called pups, although some people call them kits. Foxes and vixens mate for life. But life for arctic foxes is short. Most die before they are five years old, although a few live as long as ten years.

In February or March, the fox and the vixen mate. A couple of days before her pups are due, the vixen enters her den. Then, fifty-two days after she has mated, the vixen

gives birth. If she is thin and hungry, she may have only two
or three pups. If she is healthy, she might have six or eight.
If she is fat and there is lots of food, she might have as many
as eighteen pups or even more.

When the pups are born, they are about the size of
kittens. Their tiny bodies are covered with fine brown hair.
They cannot be left alone for more than an hour. Their
mother must nurse them or they will die.

After sixteen days, the pups' eyes open, and they can see. They stay inside their den for three to four weeks after birth. During that time, their warm coats grow out. The pups get bigger and stronger.

Then the pups walk outside the den and look at their world. They must be careful. Bigger animals like wolves, polar bears, and eagles catch and kill little foxes. But the enemy that the arctic fox must fear the most is man. Throughout the North, trappers catch arctic foxes. They sell fox fur to people who use it to make coats for others to wear. Every year trappers kill thousands of young foxes that haven't learned to protect themselves.

Fox parents take turns caring for their pups. When the vixen goes out to hunt, the dog fox will baby-sit. When the dog fox goes to hunt, the vixen stays home.

Arctic foxes hunt alone, not as members of a group. During winter when food is scarce, an arctic fox travels far searching for things to eat. He trots over the snow looking for animals that have died. If he finds a dead caribou he will eat the flesh. He lopes along the seashore looking for dead seals or fish.

Sometimes the arctic fox will follow a polar bear onto the frozen sea. When the polar bear kills a seal, the fox will eat what the polar bear does not want.

On shore the fox hunts for an arctic bird called the ptarmigan that looks like a small chicken. Flocks of ptarmigan keep warm by digging into snowdrifts. But the fox has such a good nose that he can smell them through the snow.

The lemming is one of the arctic fox's favorite things to eat. Lemmings live in burrows that they dig in the ground and under the snow. Foxes have such good ears that they can hear the lemming running through its burrow. The fox waits and listens. When the lemming comes near, the fox breaks into the tunnel and catches the lemming.

In the summer arctic foxes also hunt birds' eggs and small birds. Sometimes foxes take goose eggs and goslings to eat. But they must be careful. Geese are big birds and tough fighters. No fox is a match for an angry goose. Arctic foxes only take eggs from a nest if the goose goes away. Sometimes a fox will hide near a goose family.

When a gosling strays away from its parents, the fox runs out and grabs it.

To find food in summer, a dog fox may have to go for many miles away from the den. He sets out in a tireless rocking lope. He trots back and forth, sniffing the earth for the scent of prey. Now and then he stops and looks around to make sure no larger animal is hunting him.

When arctic foxes find more to eat than they need, they bury the food. Then, when fresh food is scarce, they go back and dig up the meal they have stored away.

By the side of a lake, the fox looks for a goose's nest with eggs in it. The goose has hidden her nest carefully in the grass. From far away, the fox sees the goose leave her nest. He goes there and hunts slowly and patiently. He finds the eggs in their bed of feathers and grass. He takes out an egg and bites into it. Then he puts his tongue into the egg and

sucks out the food. He takes another egg and carries it away. He digs a small hole with his front paws. He puts the egg into the hole and pushes the dirt over the egg with his nose. Then he goes back to the nest for another egg. He takes the egg in his mouth and carries it home to his mate and the pups.

When the pups see their father, they run to greet him. They whine "hello" and try to lick his muzzle.

As the pups grow older and stronger, they go out with their parents and learn to hunt for food. Soon they learn how to hunt on their own.

When they are about six months old, young arctic foxes leave their parents' den. As winter comes they go away to other hunting grounds. They find mates and dens. By next spring, they will have families of their own.

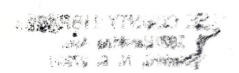